THE TANGERINE BEAR

Story by Betty Paraskevas
Pictures by Michael Paraskevas

Michael di Capua Books
HarperCollins Publishers

MANY YEARS AGO a little brown bear came to town with his forty-nine brothers and proudly took his place on a shelf in a fancy department store.

Every morning, as the big doors swung open, he would try his best to fluff himself out and sit up very straight. He'd wait all day long for someone to take him home.

One by one, all the other bears were carried off in shiny white boxes tied with gold ribbons. "Why doesn't anybody take me home?" the little bear asked himself.

Then, one busy afternoon, he saw a lady pointing at him. The bear could hardly breathe. At last it was his turn to be nestled between those rustling sheets of tissue paper.

But the lady was shaking her head. "This won't do!" she said as she tossed him back.

He landed on the floor beside a shiny pail of pinwheels. His shoe-button eyes were brimming with tears.

"Oh, no!" Bear sobbed when he saw his reflection. "My mouth is upside down."

Eventually, he was thrown into an old steamer trunk and sold at auction to Mr. Winkle, the owner of a second-hand store.

From that day on, the bear sat in Mr. Winkle's window. The heat coming through the glass made him itchy, his wooden chair had no cushion, and the sun slowly turned his fur from brown to tangerine.

A broken jack-in-the-box sat next to him, and all day they gazed out at the shabby street. But when Mr. Winkle locked up and climbed the stairs to his tiny apartment, they'd chat about the events of the day.

"I can't believe that lady took the dusty old stuffed owl home!" Jack would say. And the Tangerine Bear would sigh, "I guess I'll never have a home."

Jack would try to cheer his friend up by telling a funny story.

"Hey, Bear, remember that uppity lady wrapped in the fur of the Persian
Prairie Possum? The one who wanted to buy the antique train? I thought I'd
snap my spring when Old Man Winkle flipped the switch and she spotted

Harry the mouse riding in the parlor car. He took one look at all that fur and was never seen again. Neither was she!" Then Jack would say: "Good old Harry. I miss that mouse."

This story always got a chuckle from the bear.

Whenever the Tangerine Bear was feeling really blue because his fur was itchy or his bottom was sore—but mostly because his mouth was upside down—Jack would say, "Hey, Bear, look at me! I fell down the stairs and landed on my hat. Now my bells won't ring." And he'd wag his head back and forth to prove it.

"Oh, please stop it, Jack, you'll make me rip my stitches."

Late at night the two friends were joined by Bird, who lived in the cuckoo clock. He never opened his door while Mr. Winkle was around. But after the shop closed, he loved to pop out and tell stories through the side of his broken beak.

"Back in the good old days," he'd say, "I worked in a nice little restaurant in the Swiss Alps. I was always on time—never late. Whenever the oompah-pah band played, I liked to pop out and cuckoo along. The audience just loved me. But the big bass drummer was jealous, and one night he whacked me in the beak with his big bass drum stick."

"Please don't make me laugh," the Tangerine Bear would cry as tears ran down his cheeks. "My face won't dry for a week."

And that's the way it was until they heard Mr. Winkle's key in the lock. He'd hang up his coat and say, "Good morning, little ones," and another day would begin. Another sun would climb the side of the sky—except when it rained, of course—and the world turned around and the years went by.

It was snowing one evening when the Tangerine Bear saw a stranger peering through the glass. The door opened and Mr. Winkle said, "May I help you, sir?"

"I'd like to see the bear in your window."

The Tangerine Bear felt weak. The lining in his little ears tingled.

Mr. Winkle placed him in the stranger's hands. "Oh, my," thought the bear. "He's a most elegant gentle-man."

"The little fellow's mouth is upside down," the stranger said.

"That's it," thought the Tangerine Bear. "It's back to the window. I'm doomed to spend the rest of my days with itchy fur, a sore bottom, and no home."

But the stranger continued. "How much are you asking for him?"

"I really don't know!" said Mr. Winkle. "No one ever asked before."

"Well, this little bear is worth quite a bit of money because his mouth is upside down. I'll give you two hundred if you throw in the jack-in-the-box."

"Dollars?" gasped Mr. Winkle.

"Yes, dollars."

Mr. Winkle began pacing up and down, muttering, "I could use the money. The rent is due."

"Foolish old man, say something," thought the bear. "I'll *never* have another chance to find a home."

"I'm sorry, sir," said Mr. Winkle at last. "They're not for sale!"

"Oh, no," thought the bear.

"You see, sir, at six o'clock I'll go upstairs to my apartment. I'll eat my supper, read for a while, and go to sleep. The best part of my day is spent right here in my shop. These fellows are the only family I have."

"I understand," said the stranger. "But if you should ever change your mind, here's my card."

After the man had gone, Mr. Winkle tossed the card away. He was about to place the Tangerine Bear back in the window when he paused. "You should have a cushion," he said. Mr. Winkle disappeared and when he returned he slipped a pillow under the little bear.

"Ooooh, this must be how it feels to sit on a cloud," thought the bear. "My very own pillow, and a handsome one at that."

As Mr. Winkle picked up the jack-in-the-box, he noticed that his bells didn't ring. He disappeared again and returned with some new ones.

Jack trembled as Mr. Winkle snipped off the old bells. He was sewing on the new ones when Bird opened his door, popped out, and cuckooed.

"Well, how do you do, Bird? Welcome to the family."

As Mr. Winkle locked the door behind him, Jack cried, "Bear! Oh, Bear, did you hear? We're a family! Let's have a party! You'll sing a song about your new pillow and I'll play my bells. Listen!"

"You're going to break your neck if you don't slow down," said Bird.

"I don't have a neck. I have a head on the end of a broken spring."

"Stop it," shouted Bird. "You're making me dizzy."

"Wheeee!" cried Jack.

"Stop! It's time for one of my stories."

"No, it isn't. Bear goes first with his pillow song."

"Who put you in charge? He doesn't even have a pillow song."

"He's going to make one up. Isn't that right, Bear? Bear?"

The Tangerine Bear didn't answer. He was staring at the snowswept street.

"What is it, Bear?" Jack asked softly. "What are you thinking?"

"I'm thinking how nice it is to be home on a terrible night like this."

Jack and Bird nodded. And it almost seemed as if they moved a bit closer to the Tangerine Bear as they all listened to the wind rattle the big glass window.